Robby & Berty Cross Safely

By

Dorothy Johnstone

&

James Johnstone

This is a story of how Robby Rabbit and Berty Badger learned the Green cross code.

It was a fine day for a game of hide and seek or zig-zagging through the trees.

Robby and Berty ran around for a while then sat down to catch their breath.

“Robby,” said Berty, “have you ever been across the road at the edge of the woods?”

“Never.” said Robby.

“Then let’s go see what it’s like.

“Said Berty.”

Robby sighed, “I don,t think we should. I mean it’s not safe is it. My mum said never to go there.

“aw,” said Berty, “you’re just a scaredy cat.

“Am not” shouted Robby.

Berty stood up, yes you are. Scaredy cat, scaredy cat, “he called teasing poor Robby,

“na na na na na na”

Stuck out his tongue and ran off.

This made Robby mad that he ran off as fast as he could to catch up.

Soon thay were at the edge of the woods by the pavement at the side of the road.

“I won! I won! said Berty who jumped up and down with his arms in the air.

“Only because i gave you a start.” said Robby. “Was not. argued Berty. “was too!” Shouted Robby.

Both boys started to push each other as they argued. Robby then tripped over a large stone and fell backwards

but he held on to Berty who fell on top of him.

soon they were rolling about laughing and

other and forgot all about their quarrel.

Suddenly Berty stood up and looked at all

the cars whizzing past

“look Robby” he called, “look at all of them.” Robby stood up. His mouth hung open and his eyes wide.

The traffic was so loud and there were so many. Cars, lorries, buses and all different colours and shapes.

"Come on," said Berty, "let's run over. We can see what's over the other side."

Robby grabbed hold of berty, "no!" he said, "we mustn't, it's dangerous."

Berty pulled away and ran quickly, but only got halfway then stopped. he turned this way and that, but the traffic was so fast.

Soon he didn’t know what to do.Robby shouted to him, stay where you are Berty. I’m going for help!”.

soon Robby came back with P.C Collie. By this time Berty was crying and so confused and scared.

P.C Collie stopped the traffic with his special hand signals then went to fetch Berty bringing him back safely ."Thankyou." said Berty,

“I’m ever so sorry.

“I’m sure you are.” said P.C Collie as he wiped the tears away that ran down Berty’s little face.

“That was a very silly and dangerous way to cross a road. Dont you boys know the green cross code?”

“no.” They answered.”

“Then it’s time you did.”
He took them to the edge of the road once more and told them, “Always stop at the kerb. Look to the left, then right then left again.

Listen for traffic also for it could be just around the corner.

Only when you are sure the road is clear then you may cross the road safely still looking and listening as you go a cross.

All three of them crossed over to the othere side, P.C Collie let the boys explore for a while before taking them safely back to their own side.

Robby and Berty say, be like P.C Collie stay happy and healthy and jolly.

Never cross the road without using the GREEN CROSS CODE! BE SAFE!

The End

What is the rules of the road?

Look both ways before crossing

Listen for traffic even if you can't see is

Walk do not run

Look while you cross and listen

Only cross when you now it is safe

If at lights do not cross till the cars have stopped

Get to P.C Collie

Written by Dorothy Johnstone

Granny D Johnstone

Illustrated by James Johnstone

Published by James Johnstone

Printed in Great
Britain
by Amazon